Apes
Find
Shapes

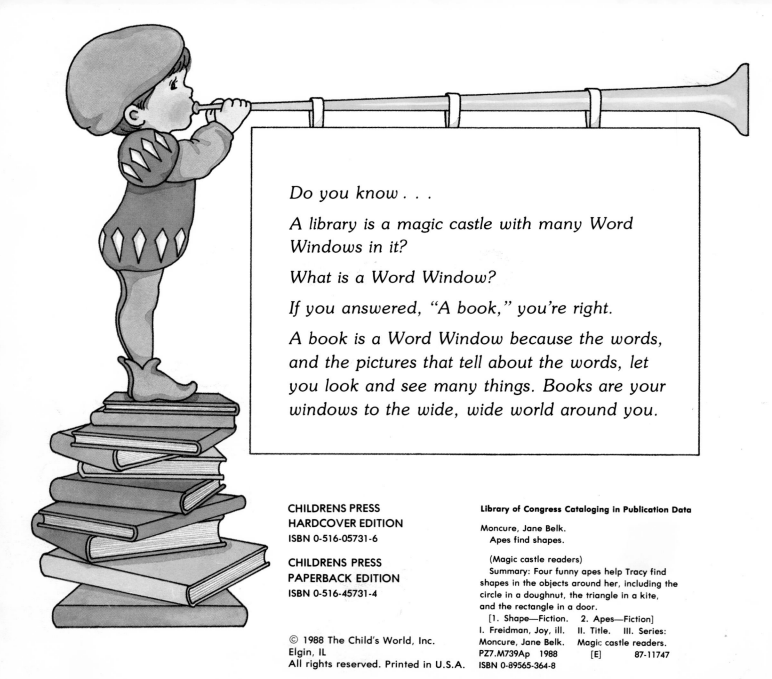

Do you know . . .

A library is a magic castle with many Word Windows in it?

What is a Word Window?

If you answered, "A book," you're right.

A book is a Word Window because the words, and the pictures that tell about the words, let you look and see many things. Books are your windows to the wide, wide world around you.

**CHILDRENS PRESS
HARDCOVER EDITION**
ISBN 0-516-05731-6

**CHILDRENS PRESS
PAPERBACK EDITION**
ISBN 0-516-45731-4

Library of Congress Cataloging in Publication Data

Moncure, Jane Belk.
  Apes find shapes.

  (Magic castle readers)
  Summary: Four funny apes help Tracy find shapes in the objects around her, including the circle in a doughnut, the triangle in a kite, and the rectangle in a door.
  [1. Shape—Fiction. 2. Apes—Fiction]
I. Freidman, Joy, ill. II. Title. III. Series:
Moncure, Jane Belk. Magic castle readers.
PZ7.M739Ap 1988   [E]   87-11747
ISBN 0-89565-364-8

Apes
Find
Shapes

by Jane Belk Moncure
illustrated by Joy Freidman

Created by
THE CHILD'S WORLD

Distributed by CHILDRENS PRESS®
Chicago, Illinois

The Library —
A Magic Castle

Come to the magic castle
When you are growing tall.
Rows upon rows of Word Windows
Line every single wall.
They reach up high,
As high as the sky,
And you want to open them all.
For every time you open one,
A new adventure has begun.

Tracy opens a Word Window.

Guess what Tracy sees?

Four
funny
apes.

"Hi," say the apes.
"Let's find shapes."

"This is an ape in a shape,
in a circle shape,"

says the first little ape. "Let's find
circle shapes."

The apes find
traffic light circles—
one, two, three—

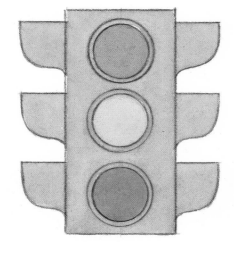

and circle eyes
on an owl
in a tree.

They find round circle pancakes,
cooking in a pan,

bubbles, a ball, and a circle snowman.

"Let's eat a circle," says the ape.
"Let's do."

Tracy eats one donut.
The ape eats two.

"This is a square shape," says the

second little ape.

"Let's find square shapes."

They find a
square window

and little square blocks,

a checkerboard

and a big, square box.

They find

stickers

and books

and a lunch box too—

and then a lion's square cage

at the zoo.

"Let's eat a square," says the ape.
"Let's do."

Tracy eats one cracker.
The ape eats two.

"This is a triangle shape," says the

third little ape.

"Let's find triangle shapes."

They find triangle flags

and a triangle sail . . .

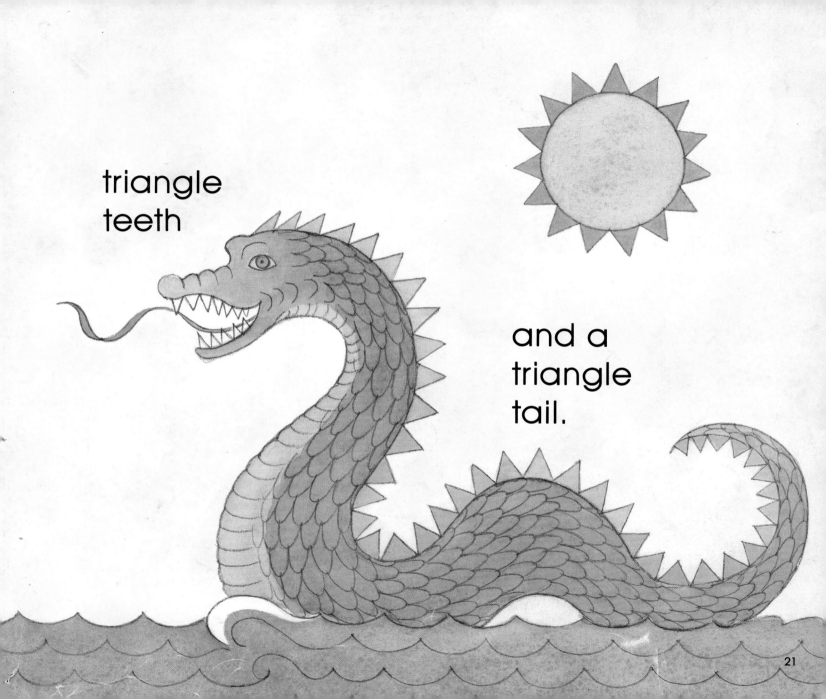

triangle
teeth

and a
triangle
tail.

21

They find . . .

triangle  baskets

and a little tepee . . .

a triangle kite

and a
triangle tree.

"Let's eat a triangle," says the ape.
"Let's do."

Tracy eats one slice of pie.
The ape eats two.

"This is a rectangle shape," says the

fourth
little
ape.

"Let's find
rectangle
shapes."

They find
rectangle
windows,

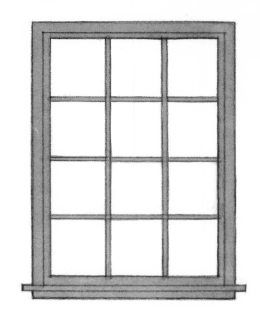

a rectangle
door,

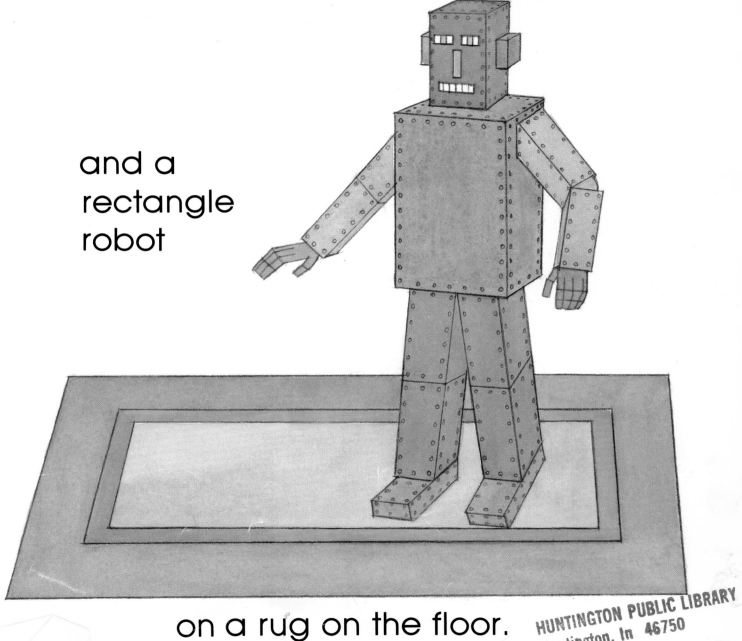

and a
rectangle
robot

on a rug on the floor.

27

"Let's eat a rectangle," says the ape.
"Let's do."

Tracy eats one candy bar.
The ape eats two.

Then four little apes
put shapes together

and zoom
away.

"Bye-bye."

Tracy closes the Word Window.

Can you read these words with Tracy?

pancake

ball

traffic light

bubbles

owl eyes

donut

snowman

circle

square

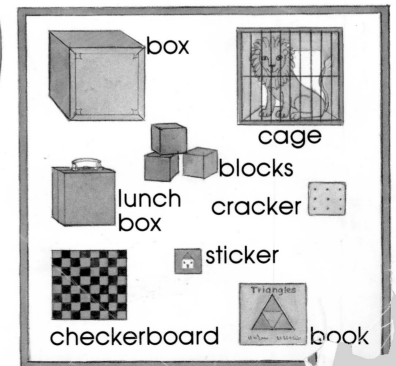

box

cage

blocks

lunch box

cracker

sticker

checkerboard

book

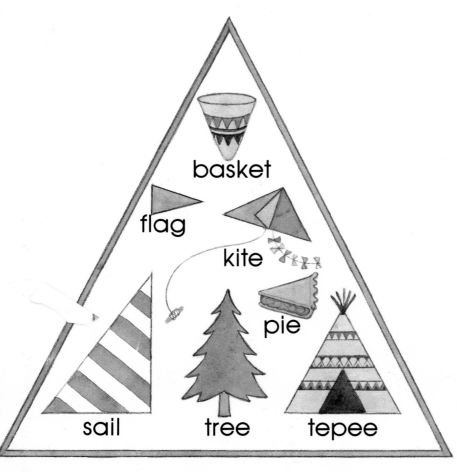

basket

flag

kite

pie

sail

tree

tepee

triangle

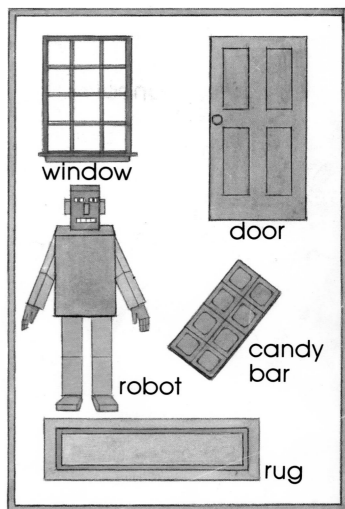

rectangle

window

door

robot

candy bar

rug